Dear Daughter
& Dear Son

Letters to our children

Complied By:

Vanessa Canteberry

Table of Contents

Dedication

This book is dedicated to the parents who need to know they are not alone in experiencing the life of raising the next generation. There will never be a manual created to follow on how to raise our children. However, we can love them, guide them, support them, and cover them along the journey.

We hope our experience and letters to our children encourage you to share your deeper thoughts with your children as well.

Introduction

Building relationships is one thing, but building a solid foundation is another. Being a parent is never-ending. It can feel as if you are useless and not appreciated at times. On the other hand, you may feel overwhelmed, but the joy of seeing the smile on your child's face gives you confirmation that you are doing something right.

You may feel you left everything on the line to make sure your presence was seen, and your voice was heard. You spoke on behalf of your child and were their biggest cheerleader, cheering from afar.

But what happens when the calls go unanswered or are not heard, and the lessons you instill in them go away? What happens when their heart has been broken for the first time, and you are unsure how to mend it? Or when you have to be the parent who has no other choice but to put your foot down, even though it hurts you more than they will ever know.

You see, there is no blueprint in being a perfect parent. There will be moments when you want to curl up and be the child to cry out your frustration of the day-to-day events, but you have to get back up and be a parent. Keep in mind that you are human, and nobody is perfect, and it's okay to take time out for yourself to gather your thoughts and emotions so you can be present for yourself.

These stories of our relationship with our sons and daughters come from the heart, knowing we did our very best to be the parent that many never had the opportunity to become for whatever reason. We hope you can take something from our letters and implement ways to show up on another level for not only your children but also yourself.

Enjoy!

Chapter 1:

My Truth

By:
Desiree Andrews

Dear Daughter(s),

Let me begin by saying I love you with all my heart. I am so very glad God gave you to me as my daughter and allowed me the opportunity to be your mother. With all that I have, I urge you, in all things, seek Him first. I'm honored when you come to me for advice, but God gets all the glory when you go to Him first. I can, and will, only give you what He gives me for you, and He only has what's best for you in mind.

With that, let me be very transparent. As you know, I've never been one to hold back, and I believe this will help others, including my granddaughters. So, please allow me to share with you some things that I know will be valuable to you all on your journey. Three of you are already mothers, and two of you have yet to embark down that path, but at whatever stage you are in, please always be mindful of who and Whose you are. When I was young, I was seduced into believing love means you had to perform, and you had to please. Deep down somewhere, I knew that was not the truth, but I wanted to *feel* something; I wanted to feel loved. It was not the guy, or I should say guys, who seduced me but the enemy, old slew foot himself, Satan. But I kept up the allusion and entered motherhood at a young age.

I was, as they say, young, dumb, and in love, or so I thought. I'll be honest and say, "*I got* pregnant for all the wrong reasons"; however, that did not diminish the love I had to give you, my first-born child. I loved you from day *minus* one. I had hoped that your entrance into this world would bring me all the things I wanted in life, one of those being a loving family. Instead, I put you through some things that no child should have to endure. You were young and may not be able to remember everything, but I see many things affected you and stuck with you as you grew older. For *that*, I sincerely apologize. Things did not work out with your biological father and I, but I am grateful that God brought a man in our lives who loves us unconditionally. He has raised you as his own and loved you just as much. He was, and is, able to do that because he loves God more than he does anything or anyone else, and that's a good thing.

So, I say to you, my daughter(s), love God and trust Him to send the right man in your life. He will do it, and when He does, you *will* know it as well—*if* you have cultivated a

4

relationship with Him. This is what I want you all to do; cultivate, build, and maintain your relationship with God and allow Him to bring you through; allow Him to show you all things and give you the love and happiness you so deserve. You are His child, and He loves you unconditionally. So, this is what you look for in a man; one who loves God more than you. And don't be offended by that because if that be the case, He will love you and treat you good.

OK, some of you know my story, but allow me to relive it with you with the eyes, knowledge, and understanding I now have. I see so much of me in y'all, and all I can do is pray for you and ask God to keep you. You know my mom died when I was three, and I was raised by Grandma Cutie, even though Dad lived in the same city and eventually remarried. That was something they worked out after Mom passed.

I can understand Dad's point of view; he was a young widower and father. I'm sure my mom, being young herself, spent the majority of time with me; not that my dad wasn't there, but understand the era I grew up in: women took care of the children and household, and men worked. Not saying this was absolutely the case because there were, of course, working women, but it was just more common for women to stay home and take care of the household. I know it was a bit different with my parents because I do know my mom was a dental hygienist, or going to school for it, and at some point, she worked in their grocery store. I know also that Dad was a carpenter but also owned the grocery store and worked there. My point is, Dad wasn't very hands-on, and from what I was told, many men really had problems showing much affection to their wives, outside the bedroom, and to their children. I get it; I understand it *now*. Back then, I grew up watching my dad with his "other" family, and though I didn't understand what or how I truly felt, I can now label it as abandonment.

I felt abandoned, thrown away. I know now that wasn't the case at all, but I didn't really have a good relationship with my dad; something I've often regretted and pitied myself for. For that matter, I also did not have a good relationship with my stepmother and stepsiblings; though those were the relationships I longed for and didn't know it.

I was young and impressionable, and I believed what my grandmother told me. I spent so many years keeping my stepmother at two arms' length, only to find out later that that didn't have to be the case. Therefore, I have raised you to not distinguish between step anything. My mom died; there was nothing I could do about that. My dad remarried; he had every right to do so. Stepmom *is* Mom and should have been that way from the time she married Dad, but I was raised calling her by her first name. It wasn't until I was grown, out of the house, married, and most importantly a child of God that I came to reconcile with my stepmother; I began to call her Mom and cultivated a relationship with her. From her, I learned that Grandma Cutie had come to her to apologize and set things straight; only one step was left out setting me straight. Grandma Cutie had peace, but I was still stuck in an erroneous mindset concerning my new mom. Yes, *all* of this had an effect on me and somewhat shaped me the way it did. Early on, I was looking for love but in *all* the wrong places.

To my shame, I was a superficial Christian. I grew up Baptist, going to church with Grandma Cutie and Grandpa Rogers. It wasn't until one day after Sunday School when Sis. Richardson said something that caught my attention. She mentioned being saved, being born again. I followed her to the back of the fellowship hall and asked her what she meant. I don't exactly remember what she said, but that was my awakening, my quest to "find God." No, He wasn't hiding from me; I just didn't know how or where to find Him. I don't remember hearing much about that, the process by which one may be saved, in church. Yes, Reverend Johnson preached good, but I don't remember much except when he got excited and was about to close, he would hold the side of his face, rear back, and kick his leg up; I loved it, but that was the extent of it, and I'm sure it was because I was very young. Anyway, I had a concept of Christianity and didn't learn or fully understand until years later what it truly meant to be a Christian.

OK, so, fast forward to my teenage years. Oh girls, wow! I don't truly know what hit me. From elementary school, I had "boyfriends." My first recollection of a boyfriend was Bobby. Back then, they wrote notes to you, asking you to go out. Nothing ever happened, except we would smile at each other when we saw one another. During Jr high school, as we called it then, one summer, I was visiting my Godparents in the Bronx. There was a boy that somehow caught my attention. I don't even remember his name, but he was my first kiss. He and I had gone in the basement hallway in one of the buildings, and he kissed me on the mouth, tongue to tongue. I hadn't expected that, and I guess he knew it. He asked me if that was my first time kissing, and I retorted, "What do you think?" Nothing ever came of it; we talked on the phone often, but he lived in the Bronx, and I in Queens, so, yeah.

Fast forward a bit more; I was 13, playing handball on the side of the building around the corner from Granddad's store. The kids that lived on that block took notice and befriended me. Eventually, I would meet the guy who would take my innocence. Did I know what I was doing? Of course not! Did I have any business doing it? Of course not! All I know is that I fell into the enemy's trap hook, line, and sinker. At 14, I was pregnant by the *fourth* boy I would be intimate with; yes, all within a year. I was talking with my best friend at the time and told her. I didn't know that

Grandma Cutie was on the extension phone listening (we didn't have cell phones back then; we didn't even have call waiting; call waiting for us was saying, "Hold on"). When I came upstairs, she called me in her room and asked me, "What's positive? Not too many things that can mean." I had to confess. She asked me what I wanted to do, but at that point, I really didn't know. I was too young to have a baby, but at the same time, I didn't believe in abortion.

No, I didn't believe in abortion. Grandma Cutie didn't believe in abortion, but guess what? I had an abortion. My boyfriend at the time went with me and Grandma Cutie to the clinic. We talked about it, and he convinced me to go through with it. He said stuff to make me believe we'd always be together and have another baby later when we were older. Reluctantly, I agreed. I remember going to that clinic and being "the 14-year-old"; that's how they referred to me. I probably felt shamed but was too groggy to care. All I know is, that did a number on me; I was withdrawn all the way home. That night, I cried and cried and cried some more. I cried myself to sleep and woke up crying. Not many knew; my boyfriend was two years older than me, but he was no help because he wanted me to have the abortion. My best friend was my age, so what could she really know how to help me? It was never spoken of again, but it was always with me; they could put it behind them, but I couldn't. Eventually, my boyfriend and I broke up, and he forgot about the promise to me that we would have another child, but I didn't.

After that, I was something else. I began looking for love, again, in all the wrong places; I was looking for it in a man when all I had to do was come back to Jesus. My fourth and fifth boyfriends introduced me to abuse. Though both only hit me once for not doing what they wanted me to do sexually, it shouldn't have happened at all, but I was too "young and dumb" to understand that. I didn't view it as they hit me because they loved me, but I didn't equate it with abuse either. It was some time after my fifth boyfriend slapped me that, in a discussion with my God-sisters and another family friend, I casually mentioned it, and their reactions alerted me to the fact that what he did wasn't right. From what I remember, that conversation went something like this:

ME: "Yeah, 'so and so' hit me ..."
THEM: "He *hit* you?"
ME: "Yeah, because I wouldn't do oral ..."
FAMILY FRIEND: "It doesn't matter what he hit you for; he shouldn't have hit you at all!"

That stuck with me, and I felt shamed. My relationship with him changed. He was very jealous anyway. If I happened to be looking in the direction of another guy, he would accuse me of something. He was a few years older than I was;

according to him, his mother adored me, and of course, that had an impact on me as well. He had his own car and even had my name written on the side of it to "prove his love and devotion" to me. Yes, yes, I was young and impressionable.

One night, he picked me up, and we went driving. He wanted to go to the top of the Empire State Building; I didn't want to go. He tried hard to persuade me, but I just wasn't in the mood to go. He was sort of upset, and later he revealed to me that night that he was going to propose to me there. He showed me the ring, and all I could think was, "Thank God I didn't go." Though I thought I was in love with him, I didn't want to marry him, which was strange because that's what I wanted to get married but I knew he wasn't the right one. Again, he was too jealous. Eventually, we broke up, but by this time, my sexual appetite was wide awake.

To say I was promiscuous is being polite. By the time I was 18, I had been with 18 guys. I know because when I began to assess my life, I thought: *Wow, if it were possible, I was with a guy every year of my life.* So, I realized something was missing. During my senior year in high school, I was single and *not* looking for a boyfriend, but one found me anyway. I was on the Booster Squad, and after practice one day, one of the basketball players approached me as I was heading to the locker room. He asked, "Where's your man?" I replied, "I don't have a man." He said "WHAT!" and began trying to talk to me. Before that day, I don't even think I really knew his name. I knew some of the ballplayers but really didn't pay attention to them in that way. I had *never* dated anyone I went to school with; although a few had interest in me. However, this guy wouldn't leave me alone. I had to be at the games because, by this time, I was the Captain of the Boosters, and we had to be there with the Cheerleaders. He told me, "You're going to be mine," and I just laughed and said, "Oh, yeah." I was oblivious to who he was or who he had been with; I never really paid much attention to him or any of the other players and was content by myself. Well, he kept true to his word (which I would come to know was about the only time he would). He would constantly make his way to me after the games and tell me I was going be his girl. At this point, I was tickled and flattered.

When I finally caved and said yes to him, I remember one day after a game, we were on the bus together going to my house. We were in the back seats, and a couple of girls we knew were also on the bus. I hadn't really paid them much attention, but they kept looking at us and saying stuff. When they got off the bus, they said goodbye to me and just jeered at him. I smiled and said bye but then asked him what that was all about. He told me he used to go out with one of them, and she was mad at him. I didn't say much after that, but little did I know that would be the start of our love triangle. Had I any sense, I would have dropped him there *before* I got in too deep, but after the first time we were intimate, I decided I would stay with him. Except for the fornication part, I could say I was a goody-two-shoes girl; although, by God's standards, I was still a sinner in need of a Savior. This boyfriend took me through and introduced me to so much stuff. Between the love triangle, the lying, the alcohol, drugs, and physical abuse, for some reason, I held on. I learned about the Battered Wife Syndrome from this relationship.

I'm not going to lie; I loved him, and I wanted to believe him every time he said it, the physical abuse, wouldn't happen again, but it did. We would get into arguments and fights over her, and I would leave him or not speak to him for a few days, and he would plead with me to come back, and I would give in. New Year's Eve 1984, we were together, and that would be the very night his best friend was killed. If he hadn't been with me, he would've been with him, and there's no telling what would've happened. But that was also the night, drunk as a skunk, he first told me he loved me. I thought he must really mean it because they say you tell the truth when you're drunk. Again, clink, clink (the sound of shackles tightening), I was his and wasn't going anywhere. Amidst the fighting and making up, I got pregnant. We were still in the love triangle, but this time, I was done. I didn't even tell him I was pregnant. I told my cousin; whether by mistake or on purpose, I needed someone to talk to. She immediately said, "You're getting an abortion." I was numb and didn't know what to do but wished I hadn't said anything to her. She told one of my uncles, I think, and then that's when it came out about my first abortion. Even so, it was decided for me, but this time, neither my grandmother nor parents knew. I didn't want to go down that road again, but having broken up with my boyfriend, and not wanting to disappoint my family, I conceded. Again, I was devastated, and here comes my boyfriend, "Baby, I love you. I'm sorry; please forgive me. It won't happen again." And what I do, I take him back.

Of course, it was good between us for a while, but Grandma always said, "A leopard never changes his spots." One day, whilst snooping (yes, I would *look* for things to prove his cheating), I found a Father's Day card he had hidden. I confronted him about it, and after trying to act like he was mad because I found it, he told me she and her friend bought some weed so he and his friend could get high with them, and it just happened. I told him this time I was done. "She won; go back to her." He pleaded with me not to leave him and refused to let me leave his house, which of course brought on another fight. After fighting to leave his house, I told him I would stay with him on one condition that I don't come second (in so many words), and if he *ever* put her before me, even after the baby was born, we were done. He agreed but didn't live up to it. The baby came, but her condition for him to see the child was, I couldn't be anywhere around, and that created conflict. So, silly me, what do I do? Instead of leaving him like I said I would, I purposely got pregnant. This time, I told no one except him.

My pregnancy caused a strain and widened the rift I perceived between my family and I. The only thing I could say I had going for me was that I was 19 and out of high school. I started my second year in college pregnant. I didn't finish at that time, but things had gotten so strained with my boyfriend and I that I ended up leaving New York and moved to Florida with his sister, with whom I was very close to. He didn't know where I was and would constantly call and ask her, knowing she and I were close. Eventually, she talked me into telling him, we reconciled, and he came to Florida. We got married. I joined the Army. We fought and fought, and the last straw was when, trying to get to me, he threw you, our daughter on the bed. That night, I thought I would commit murder, but God had other plans. I left him for good.

So, my daughters, there is so much more I could tell you, and this is only *part* of my testimony, but I feel it's what you need to know. I suffered abuse because I was looking for love, and desperately wanting to be loved, I put up with and endured things no one should ever have to. It was *only* through God bringing me out that I can say I have victory. No matter what path you take, if you hold onto God, He will see you through. It had been prophesied to me that I would serve

God; I just didn't know in what capacity that would be. I cherished my relationship with God when I came to truly know Him and serve Him, and it is only because of Him that I am here to tell the story. He brought me through many trials and tribulations; times I should have been killed or strung out, He kept me. When I felt too dirty to come to Him, He still extended His hand to me and said, "Come!" Who wouldn't serve a God like that? He cleaned me up and gave me a husband after His own heart. What I've been through is the reason I can point for you which way to go. Yes, everyone's path is different, but the enemy isn't original, and he will use the same struggles and tactics against God's people. In all that I've gone through, with God's help, I've come out stronger and wiser. That's the key; go through your trials but learn from them as well.

We believe in a close family because that's what God ordains. We believe in keeping and seeking God first because that's what He requires and tells us in His Word. Therefore, in *all* things, trust God; He is there for you. He loves you and so do I. Amen.

ABOUT THE AUTHOR

Apostle Desireé Andrews (Apostle Dez) is a native New Yorker who first accepted Jesus in her life as a teenager. While stationed at Ft. Riley, she was deployed to Saudi Arabia in support of Operation Desert Shield/Desert Storm. There in the desert of Saudi Arabia, she accepted her call into ministry. Under the leadership of Apostle Rozell Tottress, in 2009 she and her husband were ordained as Pastors. In December 2018, they were affirmed as Apostles.

Apostle Dez has birthed several ministries, including Kingdom Business Ministries, Kingdom Literature Distribution, Morning Inspiration, Kingdom Women of Distinction, iKingdom Radio, iKingdomTV, Kingdom Living Today, iKingdom Resource Center, and iKingdom Academy. She can be seen and heard on several media platforms, including Roku, YouTube, and Internet radio. She has several degrees from Associates to Doctorate, is an author, and loves God. She and her husband pastor Sounding the Alarm Kingdom Ministries and Training Center in Tallahassee, Florida.

Feel free to stay connected with Desiree on the following:

www.Linkedin.com/in/desireeandrews
www.Instagram.com/kingdonvisionary
forkbm@yahoo.com

Chapter 2:

You Only Get One Mother

By:
Andrea Pierson

Dear Son,

I hope you are in good spirits, and your health is good. I want to start by saying I love you and will be here for you to the best of my ability. This wasn't easy to write without my eyes watering, thinking about all the trials and tribulations we face together.

Becoming a mother to you was a life-changing experience for me. While in labor with you, all I could think about was: *Am I going to be a good mother, or am I going to give up?* Once you were here in the world, all those negative thoughts went out the window. I looked into your eyes and saw a rockstar that was going to change my mindset forever. No matter what you grow up to be, I was going to commit to not giving up on both of us. (Son, you will learn that quitting is not an option when you have responsibilities and duties to make sure you get things done; your personal life is different from your business life.) Once we arrived home, I held you in my arms, and the light bulb went off. I was determined to work two to three jobs if that's what it was going to take to feed and clothe you. You are my pride and joy, making me understand parenting is scary and fun at the same time. I just didn't understand why I was alone to raise you into a man. Your father didn't show up to the delivery room because he was incarcerated with his own troubles at the time. Don't hold that against him or dislike him for not being there. I surely can't speak on what got your father incarcerated, but know that your mother was there with open arms and willing to listen and learn who you were going to be growing up. As time went by, you started showing your motor skills, crawling, grabbing, yelling, playing with your toys and yes, you were watching sports. Once you started walking, you started dancing and getting into everything, but the two things you loved most were football and basketball. I didn't know why you liked them; I kept both football and basketball around, and you would play with them all day long.

The year 2005 came around. I was working double shifts to pay the bills and for us to continue traveling and save up some cash for us to move. Early afternoon one day, you came to me and said, "Mom, can you teach me how to throw the football?" I gladly said, "Sure, son" (even though Mom was tired from working double shifts that week). We went out to the back yard, and I proceed to instruct you on how to throw the football. Once I showed you how, a couple of times later, you had me go back as far as I could in the yard, and you launched the football from your hand, and it went way past me. I got so excited and said, "You did it, son. Let's try it again." Once again, you launched the football in the air; it went further than the first time. That's when you said, "Mom, can I play football?" I didn't know the resources or programs at the time and didn't have time to adjust my schedule. I hadn't gone past my 90-day probationary period with my job. (You would learn what that is when you start working.)

I turned to your father to communicate what he could help with so you could play little league football. He was willing to take you for a while and see what he could find out about the programs in the community. As time went by, unfortunately, he made no effort to try and get you into football.

I made every effort to keep you out of harm's way. However, please understand that life is like a box of chocolate; you never know what you are going to get in the box. As a mother, it's devastating to get that phone call you never want to hear. What happened at your father's house, I couldn't control, but I did try by doing what was in your best interest. I understand it gets frustrating when those

21

situations happen to us in life. You, as a young man, need to learn and listen to what I'm teaching you and implement it in your life. I can't be the teacher and do the work for you. I'm here to teach life's basic skills, motor skills, young man skills, and many more. I can remember you asking me, "Can we go and visit B2M Mentee Program with Odis Bellinger?" I believe he wouldn't have had any problem with meeting with us as a family. Jesse Cole in the book *Walk like a king* probably would have joined in. There is plenty of time for you to meet many program leaders and speakers. One leader I still would like for you to meet is Trent Shelton, a former NFL player that can relate to your story about the love for football. Don't forget; you have met former NFL players in the past and heard their story. Learn to process what you hear from people's stories, match it with your story, and think about how you can utilize it in your life.

We as humans are not perfect, even me. Growing up as a little girl, I didn't get the chance to have mentors, leaders, and speakers in my life. When I was your age, I had to learn responsibility, and it wasn't easy. I understand how it feels when there is a lot of pressure to deal with. I, too, have pressure I have to deal with as well. It's how you respond to or deal with that pressure that matters. Yes! It gets frustrating; I know about frustration first hand. You always say to me, "Why are you mad at me?" I wasn't mad. I was frustrated with the situation at hand. Every situation wasn't your fault. I was frustrated with people who were teaching you that those things you were doing were OK as well as those who were trying to have mind control over you. As your mother, I had to reiterate positivity too many times, and that was frustrating. So, again, I know all about frustration!

Being an advocate for you was a walk in the park, but the frustrating part was living in the house without you. I thought about what you were facing being at those places because they were not fun. When you would call home, that would ease my mind, knowing you're alive and well. Hearing your voice saved my life plenty of times (suicide did cross my mind). I had to think about it as being selfish and not fair to you; however, I got tired of advocating the same thing over and over again. When you would make progress, it only lasted for a short period of time, and I was back reiterating the same thing or trying a new approach I've learned from my online coaches and mentors. I was once a teenager and did some things that were inappropriate too. I learned from it and moved on to something new.

Disrespecting your elders is very inappropriate. So, the consequences I gave to you was the best fit for that situation. As a black male in this country, life is hard. We have had plenty of conversations about how to do the right thing in complicated situations. As those situations would arise, you sometimes forget what I have taught you as your advocator and mother. Out there in this world, most situations will be complicated, so you don't always have to react right away to everything. Use what you know and learn from the leaders and mentors I have introduced you to. You will not have the same outcome with every situation—just like every quarterback doesn't have the ability to win every game. It takes the whole team to win the game. So, leadership comes from owning up to your mistakes and teaching others how they can handle their mistakes and learn what not to do next time.

It's OK to apologize to the person you hurt, but the key to apologizing is being sincere about your apology and working on not repeating it too many times. Don't get that wrong; you will learn from each mistake you make in life. A great mentor I know named Daymond John said, "I need you to make mistakes now so once you reach your dream, you would appreciate it more." We as a family will make mistakes, and as a mother, I will make mistakes. Don't think for one moment that you are the only one facing a difficult time in life. There are plenty of people facing many issues in their life.

I apologize if you misunderstand me at times, but I do try to explain using a different strategy where the issue at hand can be addressed accordingly. As a parent, it's not easy watching your child go through what you have been through. It makes you want to do things that will not help the situation. So, it's best for a parent to stay calm and use their knowledge to the best of their ability. As you approach the adult life, you will experience situations that will make you think negative. You have to learn to control your emotions and stay calm. It won't be easy. Remember to stop and think first. Your thought is what controls your actions. I'm here to promote the success of your life, to watch you walk like a king; show your little brother that negativity is not the way to go. Your generation is capable of leading this country to our greatness. Funeral homes and jail cells can be avoided with the help of positive leaders. You are capable of leading your friends and peers down the right path. So, never think that it's too late to change things around. The right path is right in front of you. Just keep taking one step at a time, and you will see results as you keep working toward your goals.

When I would receive your letters in the mail, I get excited and open it right at the mailbox, wasting no time to read it. I was hoping to get clarity on what your thoughts were about our relationship as mother and son. Reading those letters helped me understand what I can do better as a person and not just as a mother because I struggled with not understanding you sometimes. We have been through so much. Not having your father around to help out made it a harder struggle, but I managed to see past all the struggle and implement what I was being coached about parenting. I reached out to some resources to help me get a better understanding of parenting, thinking there was something wrong with my skills and the way I was teaching them to you. As time went by, I was learning that it wasn't the strategy. I can't teach you how to be a man. I can only teach you the basic needs and life lessons of living independently with responsibility. You as a young man have to know the difference between being a boy and being a man. Showing you how to be a man is your father's job or the job of a male mentor you choose to be around someone that will demonstrate the steps of walking like a king.

As time go by, you will get older and wiser by the years, learning to demonstrate what you have learned to other young males that will be inspired by your story to make a change in their community. Playing football is a talent that doesn't come naturally to most young males. It takes plenty of practice and dedication to master the game of football. Some males will never master the game of football. When you find yourself in a negative state of mind, go somewhere quiet, pull your thoughts together and think about positive thoughts, e.g., why it's not worth ruining the goals you have worked hard for. Once you have ruined a step that ought to have taken you forward, take a look at what you did wrong. Come up with a better solution to the goal and try it again. I had to take plenty of steps backward to approach my goals with better solution plenty of times in my life. It just got harder and harder the more I kept making those mistakes.

For example, when I was pregnant with you, your father and I would argue about the small things and forget that I was pregnant with you. Stress is not good, especially when a woman is pregnant. The arguing kept going, and I kept allowing him to stress me while I had you in my womb. Finally, one day, I decided to leave and never return to that toxic relationship. It wasn't good for me or you to continue down that road. So, I made the right decision to channel a toxic relationship to a more positive environment because I got tired of making the same mistake that was leading nowhere. You will come across toxic people in your lifetime. It's up to you what decision to make. The other person might not like your decision. Stand firm and explain your side to the best of your ability and don't hold on to toxic people because you will find yourself being just like them.

Don't walk through life with your head down, feeling ashamed of what choices you have made, because no one is perfect. Learn from them and move forward. Don't hold on to guilt because owning up to the decision you have made will alter your thoughts from getting to a new level of thinking. That new level of thinking will bring about change in your leadership, mentorship, friendships, and other things you never thought would make sense to you. Now that you have a little brother watching and listening to you and me, it's time to put what you have learned and will continue to learn into your little brother. Your little brother will grow up with his own brain and thoughts on how to deal with life. You are here to assist him and show him the path to walk. You won't always be around, but communication is part of the journey to make a strong bond with your brother. You also will be demonstrating to other young males how to be there for their brothers and sisters.

Never assume that your little brother doesn't understand your communication. His brain is developing based on your coaching skills, motor skills, and how you pay attention to him as well. I knew that once I broke the news that you were having a brother, it would be overwhelming but exciting at the same time. It was going to take some time to realize how real the news was, knowing it was going to change us as a family. Things will get rough, and it would seem as though all the pressure is on you, but don't forget; I still have to be the parent and raise him like I raised you. Your little brother has got plenty of time to grow up and become whatever he set his mind to. Never tell him that his dreams can't happen or discourage him from being great. There are lots of opportunities to stretch your skills to other places where your talent is needed.

As time went by, raising you, my career changed several times until I got to that place where I was confused about why I was changing things up all the time. One day, the light came on and told me, "You are doing all of this for your child." That's when I chose to learn more about controlling my finances to accumulate multiple strings of income—i.e., having different jobs to deal with for a paycheck. That started getting difficult as you were getting older, feeling like I wasn't spending enough time with you, but I had to keep at it if I wanted you to have clothes, food, health insurance, and transportation. Even now that your brother is here, it is even more difficult for me to keep a level head and remain calm so I don't stress myself out and end up dead, leaving you and your brother alone.

Understand that listening to your mother at this point is critical and needed so you can learn what not to do when you have children. Losing a parent is not something one wants to experience, but we all will experience it one day because we will not live in the flesh forever. The eternal life the Lord has for us is way beyond our imagination. So, the way you treat people will determine what the Lord has for you in eternal life. You were always in to church and talking about the Lord. It's never too late to get back to some old roots you are familiar with. We all need Jesus in our lives. No one is exempt from needing the Lord in their life. As you go through life and experience situations, make sure you talk with the Lord when you are in that dark place. The trick is knowing that you are in a dark place and asking the Lord to help you out by showing you the next step. Know what the next step is, keeping your thoughts clear of negativity and on the goals you set forth before you got to that dark place. You have to be able to recognize the signs from the Lord. Understand that you will not catch all of the signs. So, walk by faith if you can't see the signs along the way.

As I bring this letter to a close, I also want you to know that as long as I'm breathing and in good health, I'm here to guide you, coach you, mentor you and most of all, be the best mother I know how to be to a loving, caring son that I know will look out for me and his brother when it is necessary. I wish you well on your journey through life and pray we never lose communication or stop visiting each other. LOVE YOU, SON!

Thank you for reading my letter. I hope this letter has inspired you to become a co-author or an author.

ABOUT THE AUTHOR

Andrea Pierson, born Savannah Georgia, was raised in Minneapolis, Minnesota. She and her three brothers were raised by a single mother. She owns a construction company, PCEI On The Move Inc. Being a single mother, learning to raise two boys on her own inspired her to become a co-author in this *Dear Son* anthology.

Andrea looks forward to meeting new people and sharing stories together. She is open to being booked as a speaker or a host at your next upcoming event.

Please feel free to stay connected with Andrea Pierson on social media at:

www.facebook.com/andreapierson
www.instagram.com/andreapierson
www.mspierson29@gmail.com

Chapter 3:

My Pride & Joy

By:
Gwen Brown

Dear Peanut,

The fairy tales that we read together paint pictures of happy endings and perfect worlds. Real-life is not like those fairy tales; you will have many great days, but you will also have your fair share of bumps and bruises. In your formative years, I am leading, correcting, and speaking to you honestly because I want to equip you with the tools and direction to navigate through your journey called life. As a mother, I would love to take every obstacle out of your path, absorb every hurt you may feel, and be your sounding board for life. Unfortunately, that is unrealistic. Everything will not be favorable to you. You will endure hardship that will make you feel like life is over, and your trials may even make you feel like giving up. Quitting is not an option for you because you are made for success. You will have to find the strength to endure every obstacle that comes your way. In life, you will need to save for a rainy day; this includes finances, relationships, and resources. Finally, your ability to communicate effectively will be invaluable to you.

Growing up, my parents did not equip me with financial literacy; therefore, I want to give you the keys to financial success. The first step in financial success is to effectively create several streams of income. Never depend on one source for financial stability because it can be taken away from you in a whim. In the world we live in, access to finances is necessary, so save! Save! Save! At every income bracket you reach, create a budget that includes saving, paying your bills, and discretionary necessities. Once your budget is created, stick to it! Don't think that it is necessary to buy high-priced items that do not give you any return on your money, i.e., cars, clothes, and accessories. Most high-priced items loose value immediately; therefore, they do not add value to your bottom line. These high-priced items will only bring you temporary happiness and do not justify the value when you need to access funds immediately. If you feel the need to have those things, research them and save for them. Do not spend on impulse or because you have the funds readily available. Obtaining these high-priced items when you do not have significant savings is living above your means, which is a direct path to debt. Debt is easy to get into but very hard to get out of.

By having several streams of income, you will always have a reservoir of funds. Therefore, cash will always be available to you. Pay all your bills on or before the due date. This will improve and maintain your credit score. If you feel that you will fall behind, call your creditors prior to the bill's due date and discuss the situation and ask for help. Lenders and creditors have programs that will assist you in troubling times to keep your credit score intact. There is no real need for multiple credit cards. Obtain one credit card that you can use for emergency spending. At the end of each month, pay the entire balance of the card if possible. If paying the entire balance of the card is not reasonable, create a plan where the balance can be paid within a reasonable time, before using the card, without obtaining high-interest rates on the balance. Never be a co-signer for anyone else's debt; if they stop making payments, you will be responsible for the repayment of their loan. Do not lend money to anyone: 1) if you cannot afford it, 2) the person has proven to be financially irresponsible, and 3) the person cannot reciprocate the loan if you were in need. Invest your money in stocks and projects that will provide a significant return on your investment. You can operate effectively in knowing that I am building a foundation that will not require you to be financially responsible for anything until you are of age. Once you are of age, you will be allowed to live under my roof until you feel the need to spread your wings. I will always be your resource.

As your mother, it is my goal to expose you to as much as possible: music, travel, reading, dancing, and sports. Exposing you to these things will help form your passions, spark your interest, allowing you to get to know you. These interactions are important because, in life, you will need to know who you are and be assured in your path and the steps that you are taking. If you don't know you and are not confident on your path, you will be let down and disappointed in individuals. Individuals will pose as friends and insist that they want the best for you, but their actions and words will differ. You will have to learn the power of discernment to understand who you should have around you. In the same respect, along your path, you will need to build relationships. In this day and age, it is important to build relationships because everyone that you come in contact with is a potential alliance—treat them as such. Never ruin (purposely) your relationships. You will need to possess the skills of compartmentalizing each relationship.

Compartmentalizing these relationships based on your life needs will help you address them accordingly. It is important to build and maintain relationships because you never know where your path may lead you. On your journey, you may need to use the relationship to propel you to the next level. Thoroughly understanding your relationships may be a thin line; you must be careful not to be selfish and consider others' feelings and long-term effects in all your interactions personally and professionally. You will need to keep pure, genuine, positive people around you. These people will keep you on the right path, challenge you, and elevate you on your path. Remember, one decision or action can negatively or positively affect you for the rest of your life. Therefore, it is important to be steadfast and thoughtful in your decision making, regardless of the situation.

Being a female in a man-centric world will be hard to navigate. All governing rules in most of the interactions you may encounter have been historically and will be dominated by men. Additionally, African American females are disrespected, treated as inferior, and broken down in every possible way. You are considered weak because you are a female. The color of your skin is an additional hindrance because others view your color as inferior. Our world has generational scars that are not your fault, but you will have to deal with the effects of them.

I want you to know that you are more than enough. You are perfect from head to toe, and nothing in this world will ever change that. God came so that you may have life and have it more abundantly. You only have one life; therefore, you do not have to be restricted based on others' assumptions and misconceptions. As an African American woman, you have the unacknowledged tasks of being present, effective, and memorable, all of which you have the innate power within you. Because you have these "special powers," when you walk into a room ... command it! You deserve your seat at the table along with everyone else. Speak up, explain, and detail as many as necessary until you are heard; your voice is necessary. In all that you do, be true to yourself. Never reduce yourself to adhere to someone else's standards or to compromise your beliefs.

There may be times when you must summon your confidence because of uncertainty, but trust and believe that you're at the right place at the right time. There are many paths that have been established, and you have the right to follow those paths. In the event you feel that those paths are not yours, please know that you have the support of your family to create your own path. You must attempt every dream that you can fathom.

Girls, like you, who do not have their fathers' strong presence in their lives suffer long-term negative effects in the love department. These girls tend to look for love and attention in all the wrong places. Always remember that you are perfectly made by God and that the shortfalls of others are not your burdens to carry. Often individuals will attempt to convince you that love is complex, but let me offer you this simple definition: Love is an action word; therefore, those that love you put action(s) behind the term. Love can also be considered a broad term and varies with individuals; therefore, you will have to predefine what love means to you and what someone loving you means before you begin your search. Because love can happen at any time, you may not have your criteria perfected; let your institution lead you. Never downplay or ignore your institution to settle for less. Once you have established your love standards, don't accept anything less from anyone. Additionally, love is a two-way street; you cannot establish love standards that you cannot adhere to. As your mother, I have loved you unconditionally from the day my pregnancy was confirmed. Over time, we may not always agree, and I may make decisions on your behalf that may seem odd to you. Please know that regardless of the situation and your personal feelings, everything I do is for my love for you. You should never question my love because it is truly unconditional.

In relation to your father, understand that you are not the reason he is not present. Shortly after you were conceived, he told me that he did not have what it takes to be a father. At that time, I didn't know what that meant. But as time has passed, and after many conversations, I have discovered that his background was limited and has jaded his views on parenthood. We are all victims of our past, and a cumulation of your father's past has limited his ability to be the father that you need him to be. Appreciate every moment that you have with him and keep those moments as tokens in your heart; they will carry you far. The love loss of your father will not be your only loss in love. Your heart will be broken many times throughout your path, but you must trust the process and stick to your love standards. Each heartbreak will teach you a lesson that you will need for forward progress. Trust and know that you will be loved according to your pre-established standards.

Education and the search for knowledge are imperative in your success. Typically, when one thinks of education, they think of schooling, which is important to gain basic skills, but schooling may not be your path. On my path, I took the educational route, and I truly enjoyed gaining the knowledge from trained professionals. I learned valuable language, skills, and tactics (industry standards) which could not have been obtained without the educational setting. If you decided that education is not your route, I encourage you to be open-minded and consistently search for knowledge. Having the ability to be open-minded allows you to embrace new learning opportunities. There are educational/knowledge gathering opportunities in just about every interaction you have. You must be resourceful. When you are not knowledgeable in an area, you must use all available resources to obtain knowledge. Either path that you decide to take, please know the expectation is for you to perform at a high level. Therefore, you must become as knowledgeable as possible. Don't ever feel that you will need to know all things within a given subject because you are open-minded and have fashioned yourself as a life-long learner. You will increase your skills on your path.

See the world! Although I will try to expose you to as much as possible, our time and my expectations may be limiting to you. So, explore the world beyond my unplanned limitations. The world has 195 countries, and there are 50 cities in the United States; research and choose where you would like to go and go. I remember being young and expressing to my father that I wanted to go to California. He responded by questioning what was in California. I was stumped. Honestly, in retrospect, I was looking to explore a place I had never been to. He concluded our conversation by unintentionally crushing my dreams of exploring by saying, "There is nothing for you in California." His statement convinced me that I should be content in the small world that I was living in. I don't want to crush your dreams. Please get out and explore the world. There is nothing to fear. Exploring the world will allow you to gain knowledge—historical, how others live and their traditions. Also, seeing the world allows you to get away from your day-to-day interactions and allows you to truly relax. The relaxation will allow you to truly renew yourself and prepare you physically, emotionally, and professionally to achieve new goals and knowledge.

Taking care of yourself is imperative. If you do not take care of yourself, you will not be good for anything, including yourself. Always pray and acknowledge God in all situations good, bad, or indifferent. Taking care of yourself consists of three important components: physically, emotionally, and mentally. Eating well, keeping your body hydrated by drinking water, exercising regularly, sleeping regularly, and taking care of your skin aid you on taking care of yourself physically. Our community (African American) suffers from a limited life span because of our poor lifestyle. Historically and in the present day, our community has a lack of access to healthy options. Increase your life span by taking care of your body physically. Limiting your stresses and talking about how you are feeling will allow you to take care of your emotional and mental health. Depression is real, and you will have to know the signs of it in order to treat it accordingly. Depression is a sickness that is always overlooked in the African American community. The United States has policies and procedures that are intended to limit our (African American) success. While we are trying to achieve our goals, we work harder than our counterparts, net negative results, and limit our opportunities—all of which lead us on a path of depression.

Know that in this life, stresses will arise; therefore, you will not avoid them. If you have given your best to a situation and have done all you can, stop stressing and give it to God. Please know that everything will work itself out in time, and you will be victorious when the storm is over. But in the event you cannot overcome your own mental capacities, do seek professional help. Protecting your peace is an absolute must. Do not allow anyone or a situation to destroy your peace. Eliminate all toxic people and situations from your life. Having perfect peace will allow you to hear God's voice and protect your energy.

Cherish everything that God has blessed you with and take nothing for granted because as quickly as you have acquired it, it can be taken away. Acknowledge God in all your ways because without him, you are nothing. God created us to be vessels, including you, which means you have a responsibility to represent Him in your walk. Your knowledge of Him should not be a secret. While you don't have to be a Bible-toting Christian, your light should shine; others will see His light in your walk. I encourage you to read the Bible regularly; therefore, you will establish a relationship with Him on your own accord without having to rely on others. It is important that you be a good person. Treat others well. There is a blessing when you help others, so I encourage you to share your knowledge, talents, and helping hands with others. Being a blessing will fulfill you beyond your dreams.

All these things that I have discussed with you are not possible without communication; you will need to possess effective communication skills for every situation. Effective communication means that you can successfully assess a situation, offer your take and opinion based on the need. Because you are a human being that was established and certified by God, you have a valid voice. For many years of my life, I struggled with my voice. I was made to feel that my voice and opinions did not matter. As a result, I was faced with obstacles on my journey that could have been prevented if I was able to speak openly. I've also missed out on valuable opportunities because I was mute. As your mother, I have already established an open platform for you to use your voice and express your opinions, regardless of how anyone feels about them. It is important that you continue to express yourself throughout your life. There comes a price with expressing yourself, so be prepared for a lot of good, with a sprinkle of bad. Your ability to express yourself effectively will open and close doors for you, gain you supporters and those who will not support, and allow you to take a few steps forward and a few steps back. Again, I will reiterate, stay true to yourself always. Being an effective communicator also requires absolute clarity. Whenever you are in a situation where you are not clear, ask questions until you gain clarity. You will not be effective if you do not have the clarity required to move forward.

Daughter, I want you to live a life beyond my expectations for you. I want your life to be fulfilled with love, happiness, and unwavering success; whatever that may mean for you. Be confident, fearless, and smart in your decision-making. I pray that my words have established a foundation for you to propel into your success. Please know that my thoughts are not all-encompassing and inclusive and can be modified at any time.

ABOUT THE AUTHOR

Gwendolyn is a God-fearing, seasoned professional who is passionate about education. Throughout her professional career, she has been able to leverage her passion for education to groom and propel her direct workforce for success inside and outside organizations. As a former youth leader in her local church, she successfully created a tutoring program for the congregation's youth. As a credit to her abilities, many of the youth who participated in the tutoring program have become educators themselves. Also, in the realm of education, Gwendolyn has created many training aids, self-directed learning materials, and online content for other not-for-profit organizations. Gwendolyn currently resides in Chicago, IL, with her daughter. Finally, Gwendolyn is pursuing her master's degree in Leadership and Human Resource Development with a concentration in workforce development at Louisiana State University.

Feel free to stay connected with Gwendolyn on the following:

email - gwendolyntbrown@gmail.com

Chapter 4:

Our Bond Speaks Volumes

By:
Vanessa Canteberry

Dear Son,

You surprised us when I found out I was pregnant with you. I was told several times that I would never be able to have any more children after your sisters, but God saw otherwise. Your name means God is with you. It holds near and dear to my heart, as you were the hardest pregnancy I ever had, and I was looking forward to meeting you to see what the fuss was all about.

I always wanted a son, and when I was blessed with one, I would pray to do right by you. Shortly after having you, I separated from your father; that later led to a divorce. I never thought I would be a single parent again, but life happens, and I had to make some adjustments. I had to make some tough decisions, as I had to start my life over again from scratch.

I was able to find an apartment for us, started a new job and eventually got a car. I held you close to me, as I never wanted to let you go. It was something different, and I couldn't put my fingers on it, but I was determined to figure it out. After getting settled back into work and a consistent schedule, I found myself always at the doctor's office. You were always sick. I came to find out that your immune system was weak and needed to get the proper care to get it strengthened back. It took some time, but when you were back and feeling better, you were that happy-go-lucky little boy I love dearly.

Raising you and your sisters was a challenge on some levels rebuilding not only myself but stronger bonds, as it was just us against the world. It felt as if I had signed an agreement with myself for my children to be able to be okay with creating a solid foundation to stand on, accepting the fact that the support from family was barely minimum, understanding that it's okay to change the outlook of what you would become and taking action to show not only myself that it's possible but having an amazing testimony for you all later on to share.

The journey was nowhere easy. As a matter of fact, it was the toughest decisions I had to make in order to take a stand when so many chose to fall. I no longer wanted to fall and remain a statistic due to me being a young mother of three and divorced. Therefore, I was supposed to fall below the poverty line because that's what the majority would do. However, I took a route that many thought was crazy. I stood, took responsibility for my children so I can be around for you all to be proud of the steps I had to take in order to be the mother I have become today.

You see, son, I share this with you because I understand what it feels like to be raised by a single mother and not knowing your father having questions that need answering but unable to reach out to get the answers. Blaming yourself for their disappearing acts. Being around friends and hearing them talk about their relationship with their dad and not being able to relate. I can understand.

Many nights I hugged you close and reassured you that it was not you; it was him. He made his decision once I decided to move forward with the divorce. Therefore, he divorced all of us, and that wasn't fair. I was there to pick up the pieces of the missing answers, wiping tears along the way.

I share this with you, son. Going through your teenage years was the toughest, and I had to figure out how to be there in ways that were indescribable. You experienced so much loss in your teenage years than most adults have. My heart cried for help. I thought I was going to lose you due to the pain you were carrying, as you had no voice to scream out in pain.

When the moment was clear, I would hold you tight and speak into your life, support you with my actions. Even though it seemed as if you didn't hear me, I knew you did as I'm looking at the young man you are today. You opened your heart to share those things that bothered you in a way I would understand. I thank you and appreciate you for sharing your pain with me so you could heal.

The love you have for your family is something that most don't express, let alone show. You have no problem showing it, even though you act like you are the daddy of us. LOL!

Learning how to understand you a young man in this generation was one of the hardest but rewarding things to experience. Seeing you get harassed by the police for years, the flashbacks of not trusting them made me more aware of what you truly dealt with on a daily basis. It's one thing to hear about it, but it's different when you have to relive it, let alone experience it. Thank you for allowing me in your world through your eyes.

Being a single mother raising an African American young man in this world we live in is not only scary for many reasons but tough. Boys don't communicate in the same way girls do, and finding a better way to communicate with you took a lot of patience and understanding.

I remember the moment you were graduating from eighth grade, and you had all types of events before the big day. I had lost my job the year prior but was going to make sure you had a great experience just like your sisters did. We spent many days at the mall finding your outfits, and I almost lost my mind not understanding that boys shop for things that are simple but mean big to them. You never communicated to me the color you and your friends had discussed, and I was picking random things to the point you would shut down in frustration. Heck, I should be frustrated, as I could not read your mind. Again, I had to learn how to break it down more to you than I would your sisters. Once I mastered it, we remained on the same page.

The moment you picked out your suit for graduation, I was holding back tears on the one hand, because you grew up so fast, and on the other hand, I had no clue how to assist you in tying a tie. I had to be bold enough to ask the men in the store for help, and they were so kind to help you and showed you how to knot it for graduation day. That hurt me so bad because, again, being a single mother, I had no clue how to fix it on my own but had to be strong enough to accept help.

The moment you graduated from eighth grade, I already knew you would not be going to school with your friends because, again, you deserved more than what was being offered in the neighborhood schools. You didn't like my decision, but I had to be Mom and make your future bright even when you didn't see it for yourself. You loved the art of basketball and played it so well to the point everybody wanted to be on your team. Your coaches loved your loyalty to the sport and were excited to see you play the game.

With you being the last child and with me being laid off, so much change happened unexpectedly. Friends and family slowly disappeared from me and removed themselves from you all as well. I had a moment to see where my true supporters came from when my back was against the wall. It was the toughest days of my life, and I thought you resisted me because, financially, I was unable to provide for you like your sisters. I fell into a depression where I would hide because I felt as if I failed you.

Your teenage years were so tough. Although I was dealing with my situation, I had to put it aside to grab you close. Your heart was broken again, but this time, from losing your best friend in the harshest way unexplainable. You wanted to remain tough and act as though everything was okay, but inside, as your mom, I knew you were praying to wake up from a nightmare. I didn't know how to help you but pray that I don't lose you. I had never seen so much pain in your eyes. Your sisters and I were on the watch, making sure we checked on you, loved on you harder. We kept you busy as much as possible. This was a hard pill to swallow, and we are learning in this generation how to adjust to violent crimes. You were exposed to pain sooner than I ever expected. It was my duty as your mom to soothe your pain as much as possible.

But one day, you were in your room and came upstairs to see me in a fetal position, and you asked me if I was okay. Of course, I said I was, but as soon as you walked away, I began to wipe my tears away when you returned and gave me a look with worry in your eyes. But I reassured you that I was okay. I knew I wasn't, but having seen me in a position of being rebirthed through my pain, I began to pray. I prayed so long and hard for clarity of what I needed to do next in this world because my unemployment checks were coming to an end.

With that being said, I invested in myself and started my business. It was so scary and still can be but to see how supportive you and your sisters are to the vision makes me fight harder to not return to that dark place ever again. You expressed how proud you are of me to your friends one day while sitting on the porch. I overheard the conversation, and I began thanking God. At that moment, I knew I was finally getting back on track and that I didn't lose my children along this newfound journey.

When I finally got the nerve to self-publish my first book, and it arrived, you all were so happy. When the book hit best-seller, you and your sisters surprised me with my first award. I cried like a baby. I was and am still grateful to you and your sisters for not quitting on me when I wanted to quit so many times.

No matter what your goals are in life, don't give up. When somebody doesn't believe in your vision, family included, follow your vision. When negative energy comes your way, take the positive route. It will never be easy, but trust the process. Even when you have a family of your own one day, stay true to breaking barriers as an African American man and don't fall for what society says.

Seeing you with your niece and nephew warms my heart. It reassures me that you will not repeat what was missing in your life but make a better outcome due to your knowledge of where the pain stemmed from. You always stepped up to the plate to love on them, educate them, and had to be the bad uncle when they did something wrong. As I said before and will continue to say, if anybody deserves the Uncle of the Year Award, it will definitely go to you. You make me so proud.

As life throws challenges at you, it's equipping you to remember your foundation that was planted, but now is the time for you to make it solid in your adult life. It will never be easy, and you will want to give up quickly. Just remember, you are the leader of the next generation that will follow you. You will be able to teach your life's lesson to your children and eventually grandchildren you are not what others want you to be, but you are working toward what you are born to be, and that's to be the leader of change. You always see bigger for your family, so I can only imagine what you will teach your family.

We are rooting you on, even if it means from the sidelines, and look forward to you crossing the finish line when you accomplish your goals and work on reaching your next goal. Your name holds power; don't you ever forget it.

Your exterior does not match the huge heart you have. Your smile brightens the room. The love you have for your family is impeccable and unmatched. You love on me, making sure I'm okay, even when we are apart. You always show your love. I am honored to be your mom. You taught me a lot, and I am forever grateful to call you my son.

I'm always a call away. There's nothing you can say and/or do that can stop me from loving you.

Love always,

Mom

ABOUT THE AUTHOR

 Vanessa Canteberry is the CEO of InspiredByVanessa. She was born and raised in Chicago, Illinois. She's determined to continue to break the cycle of poverty, negligent, and unnecessary hardship. Vanessa worked in Corporate America for 20 years as a Secretary. After being laid off in 2011, she knew something needed to change, knowing she was a single parent of three. Vanessa was not able to obtain employment, and the mere thought of being unable to support her son attending high school and two daughters attending college was unbearable.

For that reason, Vanessa challenged herself. She took a stand on faith and changed her mindset. She's on a mission to educating individuals on the importance of transformation of the W2 mindset in life and business.

"InspiredByVanessa stands on FAITH and refuses to allow FEAR to void VISIONS."

She's also is the business owner of <u>Breaking Barriers Unapologetically</u> and co-host of <u>Motivate Social Podcast</u>.

Vanessa is a Speaker, Mindset Coach, Self Published 7 times Best Selling Author, working from the comfort of her home. She is also committed to teaching individuals how they, too, can become a business owner and overcome obstacles in their life.

Your past does not determine your destiny; make what seems impossible possible. InspiredByVanessa stands on FAITH and refuses to allow FEAR to void VISIONS that need to be seen and heard on so many platforms. She teaches you that you are more than a W2.

Vanessa is the Best Selling Author of Shifting Your Mindset and Breaking the Cycle of Brokenness, Co-Author I Am More Than, Do I Not Matter and the Compiler for the anthology Screams of a broken woman and cries of a broken man, Dear Dad and Dear Mom.

You are not alone in your journey!

Feel free to stay connected with Vanessa Canteberry on Social Media at:

www.Facebook.com/InspireVanessa
www.Instagram.com/InspiredByVanessa
www.Twitter.com/InspireVanessa
www.LinkedIn.com/in/VanessaCanteberry
hello@InspiredBYVanessa.com
http://www.InspiredByVanessa.com

Chapter 5:

Dear Daughter

By:
Yvette Urquhart

My beautiful and precious daughter,
I thank God each day for blessing me with you.
You have filled my life with tears, joy, and laughter
and so many unforgettable moments too.
I tried to teach you everything I know about life.
The good, bad, uncertain, and the ugly too.
I tried to equip you with the faith, strength,
and perseverance you need
so that you will be able to stand no matter
what challenges life may bring you.
I ask God to watch over you by day and by night.
I pray daily for your protection.
I ask God to give His angels charge over you,
and I asked Him to keep you safe and lead
and guide you in the right direction.

I tried to teach you everything I know
because I know that I won't be present every moment of your life.
I taught you the importance of courage, faith, and prayer.
To stand your ground and never go down without a fight.
You have what it takes to make it, my dear daughter.
I know that you can endure and accomplish anything.
Rise, take flight, soar,
knowing that I will always be the wind beneath your wings.

Chapter 6:

My Darling Daughters the 3Cs

By:
Rosa Morales

Dear Daughters,

I write this letter to you now to help guide us in continuing to build our legacy and so that you may know me as I learn myself in my entirety.

Although our lives have transpired completely different than I imagined when I was your age, and you were raised by a single parent, in this moment, I fully realize and want to share with you that you were all conceived through the deepest of passion and love; that I never intended to do this alone; and through the deepest of love and pains, you were raised.

My entire adult life, straight out of juvenescence, you were my priority because that was the plan. Have a family and live the "dream" … two working parents, a couple of children, a home, a pet or two. Easy. And it was. Or for a while, it appeared to be.

Our story began at the ages of thirteen and seventeen. I was a lanky eighth-grader with a mind of my own and a mouth to match. Your dad was a brilliant artistic high-school drop-out. We both grew up surrounded by hypocrisy and without our dads whom we yearn. However, your father's yearning was surmounted by a childhood of religion and abuse. And mine was surrounded by a tribe of females who did not fill the male role I desperately desired. I longed for the familiarity of having a man around for the protection, love, and comfort I thought only he could provide. I felt I was always missing something.

So I fell into utter love. Your father and I became our saviors. We were one And to remain together, we took on the world. And our world (at least mine) was family, friends, and the neighborhood I lived in. And it seemed none of these extensions of our lives wanted any part of our teenage infatuation, nor were they going to make it easy for us to maintain our relationship.

It would have been so much easier on everyone had we just given up. Give in. Heed. Believe every time someone told us we don't know what love is or simply proclaimed, "You're not in love." Yet we were inseparable.

The first time we walked down the street holding hands for the world to see was a huge breakthrough. It took about three years, two abortions, and your dad's family shipping him off to California to get away from me, but we finally felt free to love each other openly. No more sneaking around. No more getting in trouble. No more lies … at least not to others. And we wanted nothing more than to have a family of our own. So, at the end of my nineteenth year on this earth, I got pregnant. And at the age of twenty, we had our first baby.

The three of us were always together. We were joined at the hip for every occasion, every celebration, every party, every family gathering. We *were* in love. But we were still free-spirited 20- and 23-year-olds. So, baby or not, we were having fun!

When our baby was one-year-old, I made $15.00 an hour, and your father didn't earn much more, possibly even less. But our reality was, we both worked full-time. With a new child, we had to. We didn't know of any other options. Although we were loving life and having fun, the combined stresses of work, bills, parenthood, and life in this never-ending cycle that we thought to be impenetrable pushed us to decide not to have more children. One was enough for such a young, struggling couple who could barely afford the twin bed they shared with their new baby girl in her cradle by their side. So, we pulled ourselves up, made a beautiful, loving home of a two-bedroom apartment and continued enjoying our young lives—so much so that I got pregnant again.

I was alone when I went for my doctor's visit. I told my OB-Gyn of my plans to abort. He asked me to think it over once more before I made a final decision. I told him my decision was made, and we scheduled the procedure.

But he planted the seed. Not only was there one growing inside me, but now there were also constant conflicting thoughts in my head. I began to intensely watch our daughter, almost incessantly. And what nagged at me was that this being inside me was also part of her. I watched her play. She was great at entertaining herself. But to me, she was an only child, playing alone. And the thought of killing her sibling was tearing me apart.

I was torn between the commitment I made to your father and the unspoken commitment I made to these innocent babies. I knew the consequences of my decision. I knew that not terminating this pregnancy was going to terminate our relationship. I knew I was going to lose him. In one way or another, it was going to rip us apart. Keeping this baby possibly meant raising two children as a single parent.

We decided to abort together, just as we made the decision to have our first child. But as much as we loved her, we did not want another baby. But because I loved her, I was torn.

During my next appointment, my doctor asked if I had changed my mind. "Have you thought things over? Are you still going ahead with the abortion?" My mind whirled as he sought answers; I couldn't kill a part of my child. I studied her. I saw how loving and good she was with every living thing. I knew her empathy. She deserved her sibling. So as I twisted my lips to say "Yes, I am aborting," the opposing word flowed from my lips ... a simple, quiet "No." I couldn't do it, no matter the cost. And I noticed a slight smile come across his face.

I told your father of my decision and let him know I understood if he chose to leave. This was not our agreement. But he chose to stay and proceeded to treat me unkind. He took the necessary steps to make sure I was physically well. Outside of the chocolate ice cream I had to have daily, he even made sure I ate healthy. But he would not interact or speak much. The wedge was drawn. Our relationship changed, and it would never be the same. Whatever positive family dynamic we had was gone. We began to argue constantly. We were broken, and it would take years to even begin the healing process of putting my pieces back together. Years to realize it wasn't "we" that was broken; it was me.

Yes, we still loved one another. Yes, I desperately desired for my children to grow up with their dad being an active part of their lives. But those arguments, without solutions, naturally flowed into horribly ugly and painful fights.

It's difficult to express how regretful I am that you had to experience those battles, and for the wounds that are still healing, and for the ones that remain raw. I cannot imagine the effect it had on your absorbent adolescent minds to witness your parents arguing and physically fighting … every occasion, at every celebration, every party, and every family gathering.

The threat of divorce was constantly looming over our heads. It was always brought up. We were miserable. I never thought to stay to make it work. I just knew I had to go. So, we separated. I took my babies with me to try and find some peace and moved back in with Mama. And for a year, we were happy and safe and taken care of. We were home.

But back and forth with your dad, I went. I wanted it to work. I wanted a picturesque family and home. We even moved back in together … for a short three months, until we physically fought again. And this fight was enough to walk away. Although we would never live together again, it was not enough to break the hold we had over one another. Something was dying, but it wasn't yet our passion.

I thought just because we didn't live together didn't mean we couldn't see each other intimately. And even though I was going on dates with other men, I still loved and wanted your father. My desire to have your dad in your lives was an almost debilitating mistake, which led to yet another pregnancy and the unbearable thought of raising a third child alone and carrying it within me for nine months of depression and misery. There was absolutely no doubt in my mind of my incapability. And I made that fact, as well as the fact that I wasn't having this child, very clear to the world. Of course, I did not want to abort, but I was in no position financially, mentally, or otherwise to raise another child. Your grandmother, aunts, and father begged me to keep the baby. I started hearing pleas and promises like: "Just have the baby, and we'll adopt!" "Please don't get rid of the baby!" "I promise you I'll be there!" "I will help you."

I didn't want to hear it. I was already in the thick of single-parenting two children. My world looked nothing like I imagined it would as a wide-eyed grade-schooler. There is no word anyone in this world could have spoken to convince me of their assistance or that having a third child, raising it, and parenting it was even remotely physically, mentally, or spiritually possible. I didn't have it in me. So, I began a heated conversation with God.

I told God I had no idea what I was doing or how I was going to raise a third child. I told God that I could not do it. I was not strong enough. I was in love with my babies, but I didn't want another. I was 31 years old, and finally, my oldest child would be turning twelve! Old enough to legally be home alone and care for her little seven-year-old sister so I can go out and enjoy my adult life, just a little, without worrying about a babysitter. I cried and begged and pleaded. I prayed that I close my eyes, and when I opened them, this nightmare would be over. So, for the first time in my life, instead of asking of God, I gave it to God.

"I cannot do this. I do not want another baby! I cannot raise another child alone. There is no way. So, I am trusting You completely. I am going to have this baby, but I leave it in Your hands. I need Your help! I need You to take care of these children because I just can't see it!" I could not even visualize it in my mind. During that entire pregnancy, or for the majority of it, I lay in my queen-sized bed in my big beautiful bedroom and slept as much as I could through my sadness, misery, anger, fears, and tears. And I had plenty of time to wallow.

I took off the last few months of my pregnancy, withdrew about $60,000 from my retirement funds, and took off another two years. I had had enough! If I was going to have this baby, I wanted to experience motherhood. I wanted to be home. I wanted to spend time with my children, and I wanted more than the measly four weeks of maternity leave my job offered. And I was so tired. So, at the age of 32, with the realization that I had been working for twenty years of my young life, I retired for a while. And for a while, I was a great mom. But as anticipated, I had to continue to figure out life with three children on my own. And I felt alone and betrayed.

I became very bitter, very resentful, and very angry.

Drinking on the weekends became a daily habit. And weekend drinking got worse. I became the very poison I was consuming. Everything I tried protecting you against became me. I was our worst fears. As the arguments with your father progressed into arguments with you, I became the very thing I needed to protect you from. I was the terror in our home ... where you were supposed to feel safe.

Our fighting and arguing mimicked mine and your father's ... the name-calling and screaming and striking out at you physically. I was so enraged. I was so hurt, and I felt so guilty. I cannot tell you how many times I tried to curl up in a ball and disappear. I wished God would take me out. But even as awful as I was, I knew that's not who I was. I knew my children needed their mother.

I remembered my kind self. I remembered how sweet and loving I was. I remembered how much I used to enjoy love and life. I remembered how much confidence my uncle had in me. I remembered how much I enjoyed my children, and I begged you all to not give up on me. I pleaded for you not to quit on me. And you never did. It took many years, but you wanted your "mom" back, and you fought for her as hard as I fought against us, and you won. And I could never thank you enough for helping pull my pieces back together.

This journey has been a very difficult one for all of us. There are so many moments that I regret and wish I could do-over.

There are so many words I've said that I wish you never heard and never felt the sting from.

I am sorry for drowning us in alcoholism and heartache.

I am sorry for not choosing a different path earlier in your lives.

I am sorry for not providing you a better example of a father and a healthy relationship, which led to your partner choices, circles of disappointments, and energy-draining experiences.

I am sorry for making you ever feel you are less than or not worthy or not deserving of better.

I am sorry for all of the damages I caused and all of the torturous mornings I couldn't remember the night before, had it not been for the aftermath and pain.

I am sorry for giving you so many reasons to hate me.

I am sorry for the countless times I had to say "I'm sorry."

The path I chose was attached to the ideas embedded in my mind of what life should look like. When I felt life failed to meet me where I thought it should, I became angry, distrustful, and extremely bitter. My happiness and fulfillment became dependent upon the man I loved being the person I thought he should be. I deluded myself into the belief that without your father, I would not be happy … I would not make it in this world. I became a different person.

Someone my children, my family, nor I recognized. I was hateful and enraged for so long, and I was so tired of these feelings. So much so that I never pursued the thought of purchasing a gun because I knew my aim would not miss. I missed the signs and messages throughout your father's and my courtship and marriage. But I knew this time, my aim would be precise had I pointed a loaded gun at that man.

The memories of these thoughts bring sickness to my core, as there was a time I couldn't hate anything. I couldn't imagine what that felt like and didn't even like saying the word. But over the years with your father, I developed hate so powerful that I carried it with me for the majority of my life, and it grew into the greatest of contempt. And that was the force I became a master at dishing out. My pain and rage, for a while, was all I had to give, and it changed me in some horrible ways. But it also brought me back to a better version of me and closer to my essence.

Even through years of angst, I am grateful for these experiences, as they have led us to whom we have become today. And I promise our new road and journey to be a better one as we remember our greatest selves so that we may surrender and allow the divine to experience itself to its endless potential.

I also now know with clarity that there are some things people just don't have within themselves to give. These things have been buried way too deep and left un-nurtured for way too long to surface. We give what we can of what we have if we so desire.

And remember …

Mind your thoughts, for they are your most powerful tool, and their energy will boomerang.

Use your gift of free will and the power of choice wisely.

We need not look anywhere but within for answers.

We are not victims, and we are not defined by our past.

Regardless of life beating us down and making us feel less than, we are worthy, and we deserve better.

God does not judge. There is no judgment harsher than our own.

Trust yourself. Listen to your first mind and never question your instincts. "Your first thought is always in alignment with spirit. Your second thought is you arguing with the first thought." – Terry Yoder

Make mistakes; they are there to help you grow.

Communicate. Ask for guidance. Practice gratitude and trust that the universe has your back.

Love, have patience, be kind. Accept nothing less, and it will exude from you.

It's okay to be selfish sometimes … at times it can be the most selfless act.

Plow through the fear … it is only a thought.

When you know better, you have a responsibility to do better.

And finally, "You are not two people, and you are not one person. You are an experience. Make sure you're a good experience. Now go have fun!" -Garnet, Steven Universe

Thank you for never giving up on me.

With all of my soul,

Mommy

ABOUT THE AUTHOR

Rosa M. Morales, born and raised in Chicago, Illinois, is one of a tribe of six sisters raised by a single mother. Rosa herself has raised three daughters and co-parents three granddaughters. She is an aspiring prominent author, travel enthusiast, and entrepreneur. She dedicates this chapter to the inspiring women who have kept her fire ablaze.

Feel free to follow Rosa Morales on the following:

www.Instagram.com/rosam

Chapter 7:

The Streets Can't Have Our Sons

By:
Yvette Urquhart

The streets keep claiming the lives of our sons.
They have become infested with drugs,
alcohol, gangs, and guns.
The streets used to be the place where our sons could laugh,
play, shoot the breeze, and have fun.
Now the streets have become a death trap for our husbands,
brothers, fathers, uncles, nephews, cousins, and sons.
The streets have turned into a war zone.
Some mothers are afraid for their sons to leave home.
It's a shame we have to keep living this same type of
violence over and over again.
Something has got to be done;
these senseless murders must end.
Mothers, we need to unite and demand action.
We will fight, stand, and pray
until we receive some satisfaction.

We will not sit by idle, scratching our heads and twiddling our thumbs.

This means war; the streets can't have our sons.

There is no way I will allow the enemy to just come and snatch what God has given to me.

The streets will not win this battle; the streets shall not have the victory!

I worked too hard, and I prayed too long.

No sacrifice is too great when it comes to providing for and protecting my son.

You can have my watch, wallet, cars, my house, and everything that I own.

But don't touch my son; leave him alone.

I declare that my son shall not die but live.

He has so many goals to accomplish and dreams to fulfill.

I will continue to cry out to God on his behalf until the day is done.

No weapon formed against him will prosper.

The streets can't have my son!

ABOUT THE POET

Energetic, inspiring, empowering and captivating are just a few of the adjectives used to describe the multi-talented, Yvette Urquhart. Yvette enjoys every opportunity she is given to use her talents to be a blessing to others. She is an empowerment speaker extraordinaire, clean comedienne, poet, writer and actress. Yvette travels all over the state of Virginia, North Carolina and beyond using her God given abilities to empower, bring laughter, love, joy, hope and inspiration wherever she goes. As much as she loves inspiring others and entertaining, nothing is more rewarding or gives her as much satisfaction as being the mother of three beautiful daughters; Endia, Jamyrah and Chelsea and a wife to James Urquhart. Yvette enjoyed a career with Nationwide Insurance Company for 23 years; however, with the genuine love and passion that she has for people, she knew that there was an even greater purpose and plan that God has for her life. It took a couple of years of hesitation and fear before she decided to take a leap of faith and pursue her childhood dream of becoming an empowerment speaker and successful entertainer in which she would stir up the gifts that God has given her and use them to bless men, women, boys and girls everywhere!

Yvette has a way of capturing the attention of the audience whether she is delivering an empowering message as a keynote speaker or arresting their attention while performing an original poetry piece. Yvette is a published poet and also received the honor of distinguished poet from the National Library of Poetry. As a clean comedienne, Yvette is the creator of her inspirational, sensational and hilariously funny alter ego, Hassie Mae Collins Smith Higginbotham Brown, affectionately known as "Ms. Hassie Mae." Yvette feels right at home on stage as she has written several plays and has also enjoyed being part of the cast of several local plays. One of her plays, "Journey of Faith from the Slave House to the White House," aired on our local station, Channel CW5 and the hit stage play, "Mama's Pearls," landed her on stage at the Black Theatre Festival in Washington, DC.

Yvette resides in Long Island, VA where she is immensely involved in her community and seeks out every opportunity to serve and use her God given abilities to bless and be a blessing. She is a member of the Minority Council for Gretna Middle School. Yvette is a member of the board for the Bridge Community Center in Gretna, VA where she also helps tutor students in their after school program. She is also a volunteer/group leader at the local domestic violence shelter, Frannie's House, where she inspires, encourages, trains, empowers and provides emotional support to victims and survivors of domestic violence. She is a junior at Liberty University where she is pursuing a Bachelor's in Communication. She is employed part-time through Liberty's school of Osteopathic Medicine. Yvette enjoys making individuals feel their own kind of beautiful as a Mary Kay Independent Beauty Consultant. Yvette is extremely active in her church where she serves as a table leader in the Women's ministry, story teller in the children's ministry and volunteers during Vacation Bible School. Yvette is founder of Stir Up the Gift Ministry and co-founder of Sisters of Strength International Women's Ministry. Yvette has a sincere heart and love for children of all ages and works with Pastor Kell & First Lady Paulette Stone of Gospel Tabernacle Outreach Center in Gretna, VA as the coordinator of their youth ministry; Kingdom Kids, a church for kids in grades K-12.

Yvette is very humbled for the gifts she has been given and is convinced that her assignment and purpose is to share them with everyone she is fortunate enough to come in contact with along life's journey. Yvette is a lover of life and believes in unleashing the best her everyday. She is dedicated to living life to the fullest so that she can die empty having given every part of herself to loving, helping, empowering, impacting and serving others. If she can do this, then she believes she will have fulfilled God's divine plan for her life.

Feel free to connect with Yvette Urquhart on the following:

www.Instragram.com/EmbraceLifeWithYvette

www.Facebook.com.EmbraceLifeWithYvette

Chapter 8:

You Hold the Power

By:
Vanessa Canteberry

Dear Daughters,

I would write you letters when you were little, never knowing when or if I would give them to you. But then God provides a bigger picture, and now it's formed into a book—something you can share with your children. But most importantly, have insight into a deeper level of my thoughts and prayers for you.

I would spend a lot of alone time, mapping out a plan to make your life matter, to not allow my upbringing to disrupt your experience with having me as your mom. Never in my wildest dreams did I ever think that I would end up a single mom, let alone my children becoming my sole family, even though I have a bloodstream of individuals that carried the same name; just not the same outlook on life. It's okay; I had to accept it and not allow it to become my shortcoming of making another excuse as to why I can not equip you with the tools you need to survive in this space we call our world.

I shared my story with you, but sometimes, I feel it's time for me to share the thoughts I would write in the letters that I would tuck away and find when I am on a search for something.

Being a teen mom, I was unsure if I would survive to see you become something that I knew would be absolutely amazing. I had no direction and was lost for many reasons and hoping to be found again. But it took a lot of me to be honest with myself and to be willing to surrender to be open to receiving something new in my life, which was positive people around me.

It was hard for me to open up, and I had no clue who I could trust. I was violated in so many ways, and I wanted to make sure I don't make the same decision with you. I understood that I was your voice, your confidant, and the person you depended on. So, how to work on me and still be able to mold you was my biggest challenge.

Growing up so fast, I missed a lot of steps, so I had to go back to the drawing board to start over, to learn my true identity, to remove those things that left me broken, to be willing to show you a better version of myself while I continued to work on me. It was not easy, but I needed to be the parent that I didn't get to know but wanted to meet;

however, at the same time, accepting that it's impossible to undo the decisions that had been made.

I prayed over you while you were sleeping, even when you woke up, when you would walk past my room and even in the car ride before you went to school. I prayed that I would be present to see you grow into the princess I grew to love on a deeper level. I prayed you would love me when I didn't know if I was doing it right but giving you my all. I had to make it better, even when we both didn't understand.

On my dark days, I would pray the sun come out before you would open your eyes to greet me. I never wanted you to see me stressed or even cry due to the love I so desired from my family. I had to accept my family was depending on me to be their superwoman even when I didn't have a cape.

Thank you for the journey. I would spend so much time on my knees because I knew I had to give it my all so I can live long enough so you can stand on your own. I know the history of my family, and it's not cohesive to what I work so hard to instill in you. I moved you to areas that offered not only better schools but a culture mix. Even when I didn't know how I would pay the bills for the area we lived in, it was vital to show you different, to let you see that you deserved the same education as the other races, play in parks that didn't have violence on every corner, learn other languages, experience the things I didn't experience but was willing to learn through you.

Being a parent is a blessing in itself. Having life-uttering, challenging decisions to make is sometimes unavoidable. However, you want to make sure you are putting all your effort, support, and knowledge in raising your children to the utmost regardless if we experienced the best of school, upbringing, neighbor, or even family.

The world we live in today makes it even harder, as there are very few support systems in and out of the family we can depend on. Therefore, a lot falls on one part the majority of the time to pick up the pieces and just to make ends meet.

Girls, you were the beginning of change in my life. You provided me with eyes to see things clearer. A shift in my mindset to do better. Regardless of me being a teen mom, I knew I had to do better by you. Being honest with my upbringing and seeking ways to make your life better was on my vision board. With no blueprint, I always held onto hope. Hope in knowing that anything is possible.

Being the firstborn, we had to grow together. I was your shield, protecting you from all types of danger that could possibly come your way. I wanted to make sure you felt genuine love. Your smile lit up the room, and then you had quick combat remarks to match. You caught on really quick. I could show you something once, and you would put a puzzle together in no time. Education was big to me, so I made sure you went to daycares that taught you something. Then I would stay consistent to make sure you were learning more when you were at home.

We didn't have much, so I used the time we had to instill value in you, always telling you how pretty and smart you are. Boy you took that and ran with it. You always received the honor roll in school. You didn't have to study much and would be the last to turn in your assignments. You knew how to drive me nuts. LOL!

You loved teaching your siblings things you learned in school and had an interesting way of breaking things down to their understanding. When you were focused, you would manifest your thought in your writing or artwork.

Teenage years were tough, especially when you became pregnant. It was something we all had to learn how to accept. Some took longer than others, but eventually, we embraced it. No matter what, you had to finish school. I couldn't express it enough. You did and went off to college to explore your goals.

Often you thought I was picking on you, but in reality, I wanted you to be better than me, make better decisions than me, and most importantly avoid things that can be avoided. It wasn't easy because if it was, then everybody would take the easy route.

You had to figure out how to balance being a parent and

school/work. Sometimes things don't turn out the way we expected them to, but always remember, we can always adjust along the way. I will always be a mom that will be here, whether good or bad. Either way, I got you.

I watched you grow, and I can see that you remember what I instilled in you. Now you are passing it onto your children and creating your own. Always remember, anything is possible. Put God first in any and everything you do.

Being the middle child, you never wanted to leave my side as a baby. If you had the option to go be with your dad's side of the family, you would rather stay home with me. Lord knows I needed a break, but at the same time, I didn't feel comfortable forcing you to go somewhere to be miserable. Being the middle child is something I could relate to, and you being my second daughter made it a little easier you and your sister being 18 months apart. Even though you were so little. You had a playmate combing your thick hair instead of having someone else do it. I would buy toys so you both could play and not fight over as much. Still, in all, you two always found a reason to fight over something, but I love the fight you have for one another. Still to this day, as young adults, your bond is impeccable, and I love it.

I was totally in shock when I found out I was pregnant with you. I was in no position to have another child, and all kinds of thoughts ran through my head. Thoughts that kept me up at night and asking myself why. I could barely take care of your sister, but I knew there could be a better way. I began to get a closer relationship with God. I needed guidance because, here I was again, 17 and pregnant with my second child.

Four months into my pregnancy, I was asked to leave my mother's house immediately. I grabbed what I could for your sister and left, not knowing what was ahead. Now homeless and nowhere to go, I called a co-worker, and she asked her family to let me stay with them for a few days. I stayed there for some weeks. I was working hard to get myself together enough to have a roof over my children's head before you made your grand entrance. A few weeks later, your dad showed up, and I went to live with him and his family until I got on my feet.

Your dad and I were not on the best terms, but I wanted to make a better decision to be around familiar people; I didn't want to become a burden to my co-worker and their family. I went back to my mom's house to get my belongings. I knew I would never return. Between working part-time, finishing up school, and getting my life together, I had no room for anything else. I just wanted to stay out of the way and get my affairs in order.

My pregnancy with you was harder than it was with your sister. I had to make a lot of tough decisions, but I had to keep my daughters at the forefront. That's all that mattered to me, and it still does even though you all are adults. I received a lot of backlashes because I stood my ground to get my affairs in order before you were born.

A week before you were born, I was blessed with my own apartment. Two months later, I went back to work. I was on a mission to get my life together, to stay laser-focused to know that the situation was only temporary. Me being a single mom was not the end of the world. I needed to be the best mom I could.

The time spent was well worth it. It was an opportunity for me to know that I was on the path of breaking a stereotype of "being a teen mom only leaves you ignorant about raising children outside of the norm." Whoever came up with that statistics need to revisit their thoughts because everybody does not just sit in their pity.

I knew I wanted a family environment for my children but just didn't know what that may look like when I was in a "blind leading the blind" type of situation. I needed to see the possibility of hope and happiness again. Sometimes, it had to take place alone, but it taught me my worth even more, especially when I have daughters who looked up to their mother. I never wanted to teach you about settling due to your circumstances. I had to get up and make it happen because I knew I could not go back to my mother's house, and I never lived or connected with my own father. So, I had to fight harder to get my affairs in order.

Watching you grow and evolve into queens gives me great pleasure to call you my daughters. You took the road to becoming you in ways others did not want to see you, and that only makes me smile. You took life's lessons and made it a chapter in your book called life. Regardless, if you made a decision you didn't understand, you owned it; you studied it. Now you can move on from it.

There were moments we didn't agree moments you thought I was mean and couldn't connect. But now that you have children of your own, you've started to grasp my reason for going so hard—why I didn't give up, not allowing you to make another excuse as to why you made certain decisions, making you understand why it's not okay to go in a direction that was not meant for you. Still, in all, no matter how old you get, I will always be your mom rooting for you to win, even when you are not sure of yourself.

There is no parenting manual. Each child is different, and some can handle themselves well. On the other hand, you would be tested a lot. OMG, I didn't know if I was to be coming or going when it came down to you and your antics. Still, in all, with much discipline and prayer, we made it through.

I'm proud of you and your growth. I may not say it much, but I see you when you feel I am not watching. Keep going hard for yourself and your family. Never be afraid to become better than me.

With you both now parents, it gives me great joy seeing you love on your babies as I will always love on you. Make sure you always keep in touch with your siblings and raise your children together. Remember, I am always a call away.

Keep in mind that as you raise your children, there will be a similar situation that reminds you of your upbringing. Make sure you do your best for your children so that when they have their children, they will have memories of their own and then can create new ones.

Teach your children the importance of building a relationship with God early on in their lives. It's the key component to planting and building the foundation for a strong bond. Life will give your challenges, but keep your faith and stick to it. Your faith will take you farther than you ever expect.

ABOUT THE AUTHOR

Vanessa Canteberry is the CEO of InspiredByVanessa. She was born and raised in Chicago, Illinois. She's determined to continue to break the cycle of poverty, negligent, and unnecessary hardship. Vanessa worked in Corporate America for 20 years as a Secretary. After being laid off in 2011, she knew something needed to change, knowing she was a single parent of three. Vanessa was not able to obtain employment, and the mere thought of being unable to support her son attending high school and two daughters attending college was unbearable.

For that reason, Vanessa challenged herself. She took a stand on faith and changed her mindset. She's on a mission to educating individuals on the importance of transformation of the W2 mindset in life and business.

"InspiredByVanessa stands on FAITH and refuses to allow FEAR to void VISIONS."

She's also is the business owner of <u>Breaking Barriers Unapologetically</u> and co-host of <u>Motivate Social Podcast</u>. Vanessa is a Speaker, Mindset Coach, Self Published 7 times Best Selling Author, working from the comfort of her home. She is also committed to teaching individuals how they, too,

88

can become a business owner and overcome obstacles in their life.

Your past does not determine your destiny; make what seems impossible possible. InspiredByVanessa stands on FAITH and refuses to allow FEAR to void VISIONS that need to be seen and heard on so many platforms. She teaches you that you are more than a W2.

Vanessa is the Best Selling Author of Shifting Your Mindset and Breaking the Cycle of Brokenness, Co-Author I Am More Than, Do I Not Matter and the Compiler for the anthology Screams of a broken woman and cries of a broken man, Dear Dad and Dear Mom.

You are not alone in your journey!

Feel free to stay connected with Vanessa Canteberry on Social Media at:

www.Facebook.com/InspireVanessa
www.Instagram.com/InspiredByVanessa
www.Twitter.com/InspireVanessa
www.LinkedIn.com/in/VanessaCanteberry
hello@InspiredBYVanessa.com
http://www.InspiredByVanessa.com

Acknowledgment

To all the authors, from the bottom of my heart, I say thank you. Thank you for sharing your transparent stories with your sons and daughters. Some may have been easier than others, but still, in all, we are helping somebody else with our stories.

Thank you for trusting the vision of this collaboration God has given me. I will be forever grateful.

Much respect,
Vanessa Canteberry

www.ingramcontent.com/pod-product-compliance
Lightning Source LLC
Chambersburg PA
CBHW032106170626
46808CB00008B/2961